MW00886983

The Golden Ratio: Fun in the Sun

Written by Jen Golbeck

Illustrated by Ellie Dixon

Copyright © 2019

All rights reserved.

These are the Golden Ratio dogs
They live on a beach in the Florida Keys

Hopper and Venkman are sisters!

They have lived here
since they were puppies

The other dogs were all rescued

Jasmine and Maggie
grew up together

They joined the
family when their
old owners
moved away

Queso is named after cheese!

Riley is blind in one eye
but it doesn't slow him down

The dogs start every morning with

breakfast

delish!

Venkman gets SO EXCITED
for breakfast that she dances!

After breakfast it's

CARROT
TIME

Maggie

Hopper

and Venkman

like their carrots

crunchy

They are Team Cronch

cronch cronch cronch

Riley

Jasmine

and Queso

like their carrots

soft and roasty

They are Team Roasty

After breakfast, the dogs go outside to play on the beach

Their house is on stilts, so they ride the elevator down to the ground

They love to swim...

roll in the grass...

and play with the flowers!

Then it's nap time

Jasmine likes using
the other dogs as pillows

After nap time,
everyone is very excited

Queso and Venkman like to play chomp each other

But don't bite anyone unless they ask you to!

Jasmine likes to catch toys that are thrown in the air!

FLING!

Maggie rolls around
on the couch

Riley shakes his toys really fast

And Hopper likes to go for runs with mom

Sometimes the dogs all get waffles!

At night, they have  dinner

more carrots,

and dog treats!

Then they go for sunset walks together on the beach

When the moon is out, Venkman sings to it

Once they are back at home, they watch a little TV

When it's bedtime,
everyone heads to the bedroom
and finds their spots

And dream sweet dreams
about their adventures

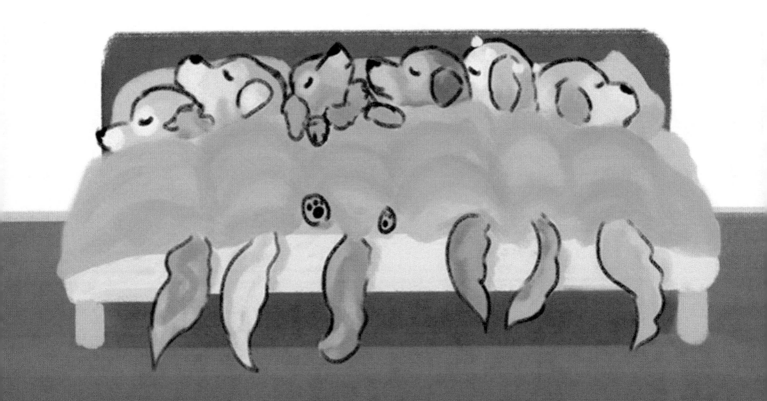

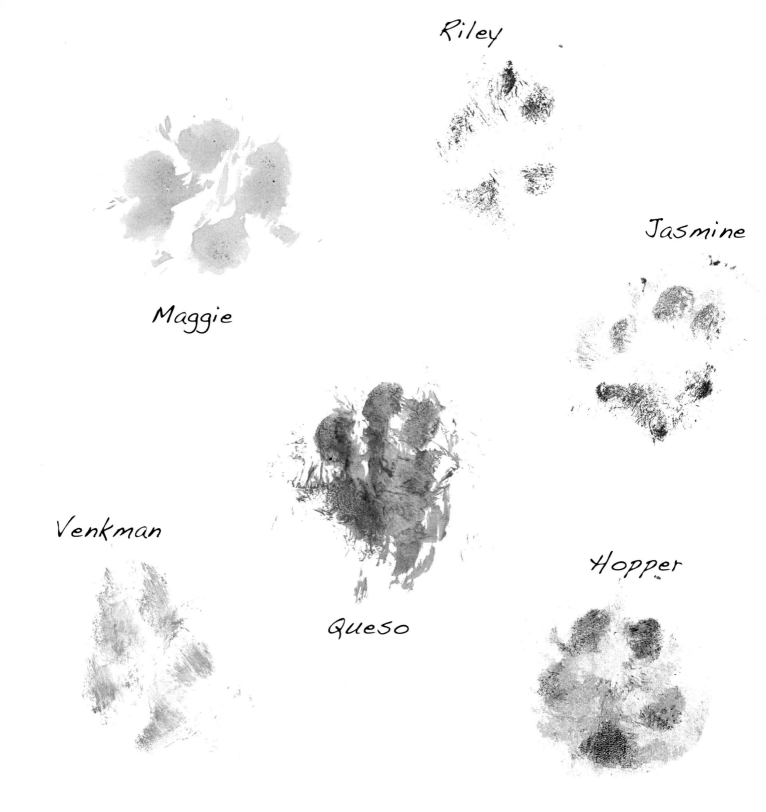

Riley

Jasmine

Maggie

Venkman

Queso

Hopper

Venkman

Age: 5
So fluffy
Happy and
empathetic

Queso

Age: 15
Loves meatballs
Occasionally
does an escape-o

Hopper

Age: 6
Total diva
Loves GR Dad
above all else

Jasmine

Age: 13

The finest dog
weve ever
seen seen

Maggie

Age: 12

AKA Schmieg

Literal angel

Riley

Age: 7

Loves his carbs

GR mom fan

Ingo, GR Dad

Goes along with this madness with joy and enthusiasm
Loves to row

Jen, GR Mom

Has so many social media accounts
Runs very far

Ellie, GR Artist

Spends so much time online
Always drawings dogs

Made in the USA
San Bernardino, CA
26 November 2019

60458437R00020